SADIQ

and the
Explorers

BY SIMAN NUURALI

ART BY ANJAN SARKAR

PICTURE WINDOW BOOKS
a capstone imprint

Sadiq is published by Picture Window Books, an imprint of Capstone.
1710 Roe Crest Drive
North Mankato, Minnesota 56003
www.capstonepub.com

Library of Congress Cataloging-in-Publication Data is available on the
Library of Congress website.

ISBN: 978-1-5158-7104-0 (hardcover)
ISBN: 978-1-5158-7136-1 (eBook pdf)
ISBN: 978-1-5158-7290-0 (paperback)

Summary: After a hiking trip to a nearby park, Sadiq is inspired to start the
Explorers Club with his friends. Then a neighbor asks the club to create a
scavenger hunt for the neighborhood's annual Fourth of July celebration.
The kids can't wait to get started! But first they'll have to do some exploring
of their own.

Image Credits
Design Element: Shutterstock/Irtsya

Designer: Brann Garvey

TABLE OF CONTENTS

FACTS ABOUT SOMALIA

- Somalia is a coastal country in the Horn of Africa. It is about as big as Texas.

- Many Somalis are nomadic. That means they travel from place to place. They search for water, food, and land for their animals.

- Somalia is mostly desert. It doesn't rain often there.

- The camel is an important animal to Somali people. Camels can survive a long time without food or water.

- Around ninety-nine percent of all Somalis are Muslim.

SOMALI TERMS

baba (BAH-baah)—a common word for father

haa (HA)—yes

hooyo (HOY-yoh)—mother

qalbi (KUHL-bee)—my heart

wiilkeyga (wil-KAY-gaah)—my son

CHAPTER 1

A WALK IN THE PARK

"No running, Sadiq!" Hooyo called
out. "I don't want you to get too far
ahead."

"Okay, Hooyo!" Sadiq called back.

He raced along a wooded trail at
Pine River State Park. It was a sunny
Saturday afternoon in late June. School
was out for the summer, and the park
was busy. Lots of families were out
hiking, canoeing, and fishing.

"Let's go sign in at the visitor center," said Baba. "There's a guided hike up one of the trails today."

Sadiq was the first one to the door of the visitor center. His baba and hooyo, and his siblings, Nuurali, Aliya, Amina, and Rania, all caught up to him. They got in line to sign up for the hike.

"Will we see any animals, Baba?" asked Sadiq.

"I don't know, *wiilkeyga*," replied Baba. "We'll see where the ranger takes us."

Soon they were at the front of the line. Baba signed them in. A few minutes later, the group gathered around a woman wearing a green uniform.

"Hi, everyone," the woman said. "I'm Ranger Quinn. Is everyone ready to go?"

All the kids said, "Yes!"

"We will walk along a nature trail," said Ranger Quinn. "It goes through the woods beside the river. Please stay close, and don't wander off. You may take pictures. Feel free to ask questions along the way."

"Will we see any animals, Ranger Quinn?" asked Sadiq.

"Probably," she replied, smiling. "There are lots of squirrels, rabbits, and birds in this park. If we're lucky, we might spot a deer, fox, or even a hawk!"

"Oh, wow!" said Sadiq, his eyes going wide. He couldn't wait! "I really want to see a fox," he whispered to Aliya.

"Me too," said Aliya, grinning.

The group set off on the trail. Ranger Quinn pointed out plants and flowers as they hiked.

"This tree is called a cottonwood tree. We have a lot of them in this park," said Ranger Quinn. "It has seeds that look like cotton. When they fall from the tree, sometimes it looks like snow!"

Sadiq stared up at the tall tree. "How tall are they?" he asked the ranger.

"They are usually forty to fifty feet tall," said Ranger Quinn.

"Wow!" said Aliya. "That's ten times as tall as me."

"Baba, can you take a picture?" asked Sadiq. "I want to show Zaza and Manny." He knew his best friends would be impressed.

"Yes, *qalbi*," Baba said as he took out his phone.

After Baba took a photo, the group continued hiking. In a few minutes, they reached a patch of wildflowers.

"There are many different kinds of wildflowers in this park," said Ranger Quinn. "Here we have butterfly weed, milkweed, and black-eyed Susans." She pointed to the flowers as she named them.

"Do butterflies like butterfly weed?" asked a young boy.

"They do!" said Ranger Quinn. "In fact, butterflies like all these flowers."

"This is my favorite," said Aliya, pointing to a flower on the other side of the trail.

"Because it's purple?" asked Sadiq. Purple was Aliya's favorite color.

Aliya nodded and smiled.

"That's a purple coneflower," said the ranger. "It blooms in the summer."

A large bird flew off a branch above them. "What kind of birds are in the park?" asked Nuurali.

"We get lots of birds," said Ranger Quinn. "In the summer, the bald eagle is very common. Many eagles nest near the river."

"Cool!" said Sadiq. He turned to his brother. "That means we might see one, Nuurali!"

"I hope so!" said Nuurali, laughing. He high-fived his little brother. "You're really excited."

"I am, Nuurali," said Sadiq. "I didn't know this park would have so many cool plants. And animals! And birds!"

"I am glad you're having fun, qalbi," said Hooyo, smiling.

The group hiked for another hour or so. They saw all kinds of plants, from different trees and wildflowers to fruit bushes. They saw many animals too, including squirrels, turtles, and toads.

Sadiq was a little disappointed they didn't see a deer or a fox.

"Can we come all the time?" asked Sadiq. He really wanted to see a fox.

"Maybe not *all* the time," said Baba, laughing.

"You can also explore on your own," said Ranger Quinn. "You don't have to be at the park to explore nature."

"Can I really?" asked Sadiq, looking up at his parents.

"Of course you can!" said Hooyo.

"There are all kinds of plants, birds, and insects to discover," said Ranger Quinn.

"Where can I find them?" asked Sadiq.

"You could start in your backyard or at a local park," said Ranger Quinn. "A field guide can help you figure out the names of wildlife you find. Then you can record them in a nature journal. I'll show you mine so you see what I mean."

The ranger reached into her pocket and pulled out a small notebook. In it, there were drawings of animals, plants, and insects she'd seen. She had also written notes about the wildlife.

"That's really cool!" said Sadiq. "I think I'll start a nature journal."

Then he got another idea. Sadiq smiled and said, "And I think I'll start an exploring club. I bet Manny and Zaza would like to join."

The group started walking back to the park office.

"Baba, can I buy a field guide like Ranger Quinn suggested?" asked Sadiq. "I'd like to use my allowance."

"Of course, Sadiq," replied Baba as they walked into the visitor center. "Why don't you go take a look at the gift shop?"

Sadiq hurried over to the gift shop and began looking around. Soon he found the book section.

"*Wildlife of Minnesota*," he read aloud. He paged through the book and looked at the pictures. He couldn't wait to explore some more!

CHAPTER 2

THE EXPLORERS

When Sadiq got home, he ran upstairs. He called Zaza to talk about the club.

"Hi, Zaza! Guess what," said Sadiq. "I went hiking today. I learned all about plants and animals. It was so much fun."

"Hi, Sadiq! That's great!" replied Zaza. "Manny is here. We were playing video games."

"That's awesome! I can ask both of you, then," said Sadiq.

"Ask us what?" said Zaza on speaker phone.

"I am starting a new club," said Sadiq.

"What's it for?" asked Manny.

"Exploring!" said Sadiq.

"Where would we explore?" asked Zaza.

"Ranger Quinn said we can explore anywhere," said Sadiq. "I bought a field guide too."

"I'm in," said Zaza.

"Me too!" said Manny. "What's the name of our newest club?"

"The Explorers Club!" said Sadiq.

After Sadiq hung up, he went downstairs for a snack. Hooyo was in the living room on the computer.

"What are you doing, Hooyo?" asked Sadiq.

"The Fourth of July is next weekend," Hooyo explained. "I'm sending out an invitation to our neighborhood block party."

"Like the one we had last year?" asked Sadiq.

Hooyo nodded, smiling. "*Haa*, qalbi," she said.

Sadiq loved block parties. Zaza and Manny both lived nearby, so they were usually there too. "I can't wait!" he said.

* * *

The next day, the Explorers Club met at the neighborhood playground to plan their new club.

"I brought notebooks from home for us," said Sadiq. He passed one to each of his friends. "We can use them as nature journals."

"Can we draw pictures of what we see?" asked Zaza.

"Yes," said Sadiq. "You can draw what you see and then make notes about it."

"How will we know what we are seeing?" asked Manny.

"That's what the field guide is for!" said Sadiq. He held the book out for them to see. "It has pictures of the plants and animals nearby. It also tells you about what they look like, where they live, and what they need to survive."

"Cool!" said Zaza. He took the field guide from Sadiq and began to look through it.

Just then, two of their other friends walked onto the playground.

"Hi, Lena! Hi, Anna!" called Sadiq. He waved them over. "Come hang out with us!"

"Hi, guys!" said the girls, walking toward them. "What are you up to?"

"We are about to go exploring," said Zaza. "Do you want to join us?"

"Exploring what?" asked Lena.

"Plants and animals," said Manny. "We started a new club—the Explorers Club!"

"Sadiq has a field guide. We thought it would be fun to try to use it here," said Zaza. He handed the field guide to Lena.

"That sounds like lots of fun," said Anna.

"Look at the cute bunny!" Lena said, looking through the field guide. She turned to Anna. "Let's join the Explorers Club!"

"Where should we start?" asked Anna. "Should we look for flowers or animals?"

"Let's look for animals first," said Sadiq. "They are way cooler."

"What kind of animals?" asked Lena. She handed the field guide back to Sadiq.

"There are deer nearby. I'd like to see one," said Sadiq.

"Cool!" the kids replied.

They walked toward the trees to search for animals.

"Look, a butterfly!" said Lena. The orange butterfly was resting on a bush.

"It's really pretty," said Anna.

"Can we look up its name?" asked Zaza.

"Yes," said Sadiq. He opened his field guide to check.

Manny looked over Sadiq's shoulder. "It's a painted lady butterfly," he said.

"I don't think that's right," said Anna, peering at the page. "The one you're looking at in the book has spots. This one has stripes. Look at the wings."

"It's a monarch butterfly," said Zaza, looking at the book. "Look at the picture here. It looks exactly the same."

Just then, the butterfly flapped its wings and took off.

"It flew away!" said Anna, smiling. "Maybe it went to find flowers somewhere else."

"Let's look for bigger animals," said Manny. "I'd like to see a deer too. Where do we look, Sadiq?"

Sadiq flipped through the pages of his field guide. "It says they live near forests and farmland."

Sadiq frowned. "There are no farms near here, but there is a forest." He pointed to the trees in the distance.

"Let's go!" said Anna.

"I'm not allowed to leave the park," said Sadiq. "But we can look along the edges of the trees."

The kids kept exploring and looking for animals at the edge of the woods. Still, they only found plants and insects.

"I am getting tired," said Sadiq, sighing. "We still haven't found any cool animals. Just insects."

"Should we go home?" asked Manny. "I am pretty tired too." He leaned against a tree.

Just then, there was a rustling noise behind them in the woods. The kids all went quiet and listened closely to the sound.

A moment later, a squirrel poked its head out from behind a bush.

"Ugh! I thought it was going to be a deer!" said Zaza.

"Me too," said Lena, laughing.

"Let's go home," said Anna. "We can try again tomorrow."

The kids headed back toward the playground.

Suddenly Zaza bent down to look at something. "Come and look at this flower," he said. "It's such a bright color!"

"Is it a wood lily?" asked Lena, flipping through the book.

"I think that's too red," said Sadiq, looking at the picture. "Zaza's flower is not as red."

Lena continued to look through the book. She finally stopped on a page. "I found it!" she shouted. "I think it's a red columbine."

She held up the field guide to show the others.

"Lena's right," said Zaza, looking
from the book to the flower. "The
picture matches the flower exactly!"

"The Explorers are back!" said Sadiq,
laughing.

CHAPTER 3

MEETING MS. MAGEE

The next morning, the kids met at the park again. "Let's check out the creek," said Zaza, walking toward it. "Maybe there are turtles in it."

"Or frogs. Ribbit! Ribbit!" said Manny.

"Everyone, please be careful," said Sadiq. "Don't fall in the water! My hooyo says the creek can be really deep."

"Oh! A ladybug," said Lena, kneeling on the grass. "Anna, come look!"

"We'll look by the shore," said Manny.

"Call us over if you find something," said Lena. "We can look in the field guide and write it down."

"Is that a turtle?" asked Sadiq, staring at something in the water.

"No, that's a rock," said Manny, laughing.

"I found a frog!" shouted Zaza, who was a little way down the shore.

The Explorers all made their way toward Zaza.

"Let's check the field guide and see what it says," said Sadiq. He peered down at the frog. It was in a pile of leaves by the shore of the creek.

"It might be a wood frog," said Anna, looking through the book. "It's really small."

"The one in the book looks brown," said Manny. "This one is greener, I think."

"Maybe the American bullfrog?" asked Zaza. "It's closer in color."

"Bullfrogs are really big," said Sadiq. "This one is too small."

"I think I found it!" said Lena, looking in the field guide. "It's a green frog."

"We already said it was green,"
said Anna.

"No, that's the name of the frog,"
said Lena. "Look."

The kids crowded around her to look.

"Lena's right," said Sadiq. "It *is* a
green frog!"

"Cool!" said Anna.

"Look over there," said Manny,
pointing. "It's our neighbor Ms. Magee.
She's walking her dog, Atticus."

"Let's go say hi to them," said Zaza.
"I want to pet Atticus." He ran off
toward Ms. Magee.

"Hi, Zaza!" said Ms. Magee, smiling.
The rest of the Explorers trailed behind
Zaza. "What are you kids doing today?"

"We are exploring," said Sadiq. "We already found a bunch of plants and animals."

"That sounds like a ton of fun!" said Ms. Magee.

"We started the Explorers Club," said Sadiq. "We want to see what else we can find."

"We just found a green frog," said Zaza proudly.

"And we saw a monarch butterfly yesterday," said Anna.

"That's awesome! You kids have been busy," said Ms. Magee. "Atticus and I are doing some exploring of our own."

"What are you looking for?" asked Lena.

"Ideas for a scavenger hunt," said Ms. Magee.

"What's a scavenger hunt?" Zaza asked.

"It's like a treasure hunt," said Ms. Magee. "You have to find certain things within a certain amount of time. I'm working on it for the Fourth of July block party. I thought it would be fun for the neighborhood kids."

"A scavenger hunt! Can we help?" asked Anna.

"Yes! We would love to help!" said Sadiq, jumping up.

"How exciting!" said Lena.

"Is that a yes from everyone?" asked Ms. Magee.

"Yes!" said all the kids together.

"Wonderful!" said Ms. Magee. "I want it to be mostly nature items. That's what Atticus and I were looking for. Everything needs to be found within the neighborhood block. We don't want people taking things from nature, though. I will ask everyone who participates in the hunt to use a camera to capture the things they find instead."

"Sounds great!" Sadiq said. "The Explorers are on it!"

CHAPTER 4

MAKING THE LIST

The next day, the kids met outside Sadiq's house. They were going to plan the scavenger hunt.

"Let's see what we can find," said Sadiq. "Then we can make a list."

"We can't go very far," said Manny. "Ms. Magee said everything has to be found on this block."

"I brought my field guide to help," said Sadiq. The kids set off.

"We have daisies outside my house," said Manny. "We can make a list of the flowers we have."

"Good idea, Manny. We could put tulips on there," said Lena. "And my mom has some rose bushes, so that could be on it."

"We should add things besides flowers," said Sadiq.

"Well, we can't add animals," said Anna.

"Why not?" asked Zaza.

"Because they won't stay still long enough for people to take a picture," said Anna.

"What are we going to do?" asked Manny, sighing. "We can't have a scavenger hunt that's just for flowers."

"Well, not *every*thing has to be a plant or an animal. We could pick other stuff to put on the list too," said Lena.

"Like what?" asked Anna.

"We could put things like a wood chip or a rock," Lena said.

"That's true," said Manny. "I once did a scavenger hunt at school. The list included things like 'something rough' and 'something yellow.'"

"Those are all great ideas!" said Zaza.

"This is a good plan. Not everyone will have a field guide to help them. The things we put on the list should be things that everyone will know," said Anna.

"I'll start writing the list," said Sadiq. He wrote down the items they'd already said and continued writing as his friends added things.

A half hour later, the Explorers had their list.

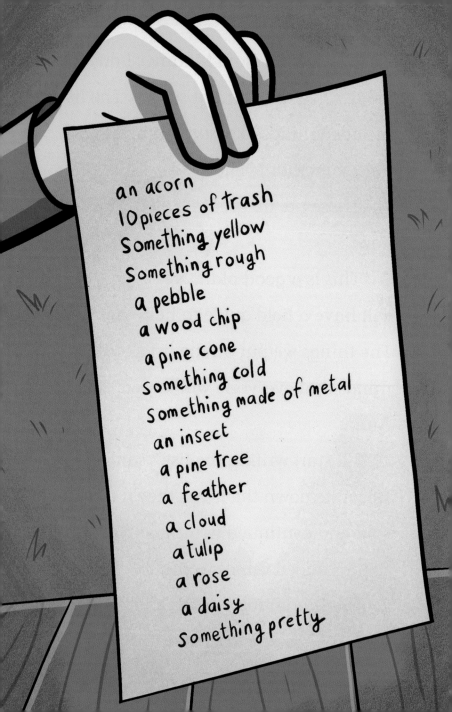

* * *

"Ring the doorbell, Manny," said
Sadiq. They were standing outside
Ms. Magee's house, ready to show
her their list for the scavenger hunt.
"I hope she's home."

A moment later, the door opened.
"Hi, kids!" said Ms. Magee.

"Hi, Ms. Magee!" they replied.

"We finished our list for the
scavenger hunt," said Lena.

"Wow, that was fast," Ms. Magee
said.

"We thought about how everyone
will take pictures of the items on the
list," said Sadiq. "So we didn't include
anything that will move too fast."

"Would you look at it?" asked Anna.

Ms. Magee quickly read the list. When she looked up, she smiled.

"This is great, kids!" she said. "I will print out copies and bring them to the party. I'll also add some rules to the list, including the one about taking a picture of each item. Thank you for your help. Everyone will have so much fun!"

CHAPTER 5

THE HUNT

It was finally the Fourth of July! Sadiq's neighborhood block looked very festive. There were red, white, and blue decorations hanging up on people's fences and houses. Flags flew on people's porches.

Kids and adults were talking, eating snacks, and playing games in the street. The block was closed to cars for the evening.

"Are you guys ready for the scavenger hunt?" Sadiq asked his friends. They all sat on a picnic blanket in the grass, munching on snacks.

"We shouldn't play, since we made the list. It wouldn't be fair to the others," said Zaza.

"That's a good point, Zaza," said Sadiq. "Do you think people will like it?"

"We made the clues tough," said Lena. "But I am sure someone will find everything and win."

Music played on a stereo. Baba and the other dads were busy grilling food for everyone.

"I've been waiting all afternoon for the hot dogs," said Sadiq. "My dad makes the best hot dogs."

"Not better than mine," said Zaza, grinning.

Soon the food was ready. Everyone sat down around tables or in the grass to eat and drink.

When they were finished, Ms. Magee stood up to speak. "Attention, everyone!" she said. "It's time for the scavenger hunt! I will explain the rules."

Ms. Magee held up the list the kids had created. "You can split into groups of three people. Each team must be back on time to win," she said.

"How long do we have?" asked a girl.

"The time limit is twenty minutes," said Ms. Magee. "Also, you must stay within the block to find the items on the list."

She pointed to the list. "When you find an item, don't remove it from its place. Instead, please take a picture. Does anyone have any questions?" she asked.

When no one asked anything, Ms. Magee continued. "We can thank the Explorers Club—Sadiq, Manny, Zaza, Lena, and Anna—for their wonderful work putting this scavenger hunt together."

The neighbors clapped and cheered for the Explorers.

"The Explorers will help me judge who is the winner. Now find your team," said Ms. Magee.

Everyone got into groups of three. Then Ms. Magee said, "Everyone ready? Okay, then. On your marks . . . get set . . . GO!"

The teams raced off in different directions. The Explorers watched and cheered.

"Kids, while we wait," Ms. Magee said, "I got something for you for helping out with the scavenger hunt." She handed them a blue gift bag with green spots on it.

"What is it?" asked Sadiq. He peered inside. "A backpack? Thank you!"

"Not just a backpack. Look inside," said Ms. Magee. "It's an explorer kit. It has all kinds of helpful tools to explore nature."

The kids opened the backpack and looked inside.

"Binoculars!" said Manny.

"And a map and a compass!" said Lena.

"Thank you, Ms. Magee!" the kids said.

"For your future adventures," said Ms. Magee, smiling.

* * *

Aliya and her team ran back first.

"I think we got everything," said Aliya, trying to catch her breath.

Soon after, the other teams started coming back. The twenty-minute time limit was up. The Explorers went through every team's pictures and counted their finds.

"The winning team is Aliya's, with twelve items!" Sadiq announced.

"Yes!" shouted Aliya, jumping and high-fiving her teammates. "I knew we would win!" She turned to Sadiq. "Maybe I'll start my own Explorers Club. We could compete."

"No one can beat us!" said Sadiq, grinning. "But you can try!"

GLOSSARY

allowance (uh-LOU-uhns)—money given to someone regularly, especially from parents to a child

binoculars (buh-NAH-kyuh-luhrz)—a tool that makes faraway objects look closer

compass (KUHM-puhs)—an instrument used for finding directions

compete (kuhm-PEET)—to try hard to outdo others at a race or contest

disappointed (dis-uh-POINT-ed)—feeling sad because something you hoped for did not happen

explorer (ik-SPLOR-uhr)—a person who goes to an unknown place

farmland (FAHRM-land)—land used for farming

festive (FES-tiv)—joyful and lively

ranger (RAYN-jur)—a person in charge of a park or forest

responsible (ri-SPAHN-suh-buhl)—doing what you say you will do; people who are responsible keep promises and follow rules

rustling (RUHS-ling)—making or causing something to make a soft sound by moving

scavenger hunt (SCAV-uhn-jer HUNT)—a game in which players try to find certain items within a specific time period

survive (sur-VIVE)—to continue to live or exist

wildflower (WILDE-flou-er)—a flower that grows without the help of humans

wildlife (WILDE-life)—wild animals and plants

TALK ABOUT IT

1. Sadiq really wants to see a deer. If you could see one animal in the wild, which animal would you want to see? Explain.

2. Have you ever been on a scavenger hunt? What kinds of things did you find? If you haven't done one, what sort of things do you think would be fun to hunt for?

3. How did the Explorers work together on their project? Discuss, using examples from the text.

WRITE IT DOWN

1. Imagine you are on a hike with Sadiq and his family in chapter 1. Draw a picture of the park, including things you read about in the text.

2. Write a short report on an animal you don't know much about. Research the animal online. Then write a paragraph or two explaining what you learned.

3. Think about your favorite plant or animal. What does it look like, feel like, sound like, and smell like? Write a poem describing it.

START A NATURE JOURNAL

When Sadiq goes for a hike at a park, he meets a park ranger who suggests he start his own nature journal. Make a nature journal of your own and record the wildlife you see in your own backyard.

WHAT YOU NEED:

- 7–8-inch (18–20-cm) stick or twig
- 5 pieces of paper
- hole puncher
- glue
- string or yarn
- markers or colored pencils

WHAT TO DO:

1. Find a stick or twig outside that is about 7 or 8 inches (18–20 centimeters) long.

2. Stack your papers. Fold the stack in half so it looks like a book.

3. Keeping your papers folded like a book, use a hole puncher to make two holes near the crease. Make one hole about an inch from the top and another hole about an inch from the bottom.

4. Squirt a line of glue along the length of your twig. Place the twig so it runs along the creased edge of your papers, glue side down. This will be your book's spine.

5. Thread a piece of string or yarn through the top holes in the paper. Tie the string so it wraps around the twig and fastens it to the stack of paper. Do the same thing with the bottom holes.

6. Now you should have a book! Use colored pencils or markers to decorate the cover of your nature journal.

7. Go outside and find a spot to sit and take in what's around you. Note the time of day, date, weather, and location at the top of your journal entry. Then, sitting quietly, watch for any wildlife nearby. Pay attention to your senses. Look at plants, animals, and insects. Listen for sounds. Write about any smells you notice. What kind of wildlife do you see? Draw pictures of what you discover.

CREATORS

Siman Nuurali grew up in Kenya. She now lives in Minnesota. Siman and her family are Somali—just like Sadiq and his family! She and her five children love to play badminton and board games together. Siman works at Children's Hospital, and in her free time, she also enjoys writing and reading.

Anjan Sarkar is a British illustrator based in Sheffield, England. Since he was little, Anjan has always loved drawing stuff. And now he gets to draw stuff all day for his job. Hooray! In addition to the Sadiq series, Anjan has been drawing mischievous kids, undercover aliens, and majestic tigers for other exciting children's book projects.